William Leonard Parsons

Reminiscences of the Life and Character of Col. Phineas

Staunton

November 1867

William Leonard Parsons

Reminiscences of the Life and Character of Col. Phineas Staunton
November 1867

ISBN/EAN: 9783337074432

Printed in Europe, USA, Canada, Australia, Japan

Cover: Foto ©Raphael Reischuk / pixelio.de

More available books at **www.hansebooks.com**

REMINISCENCES

OF THE

LIFE AND CHARACTER

OF

COL. PHINEAS STAUNTON, A.M.

NOVEMBER, 1867.

ROCHESTER :
E. DARROW & KEMPSHALL, 65 MAIN STREET.
1867.

INTRODUCTION.

On the first day of July last, Col. STAUNTON, Vice Chancellor of Ingham University, sailed from New York with a party of scientific gentlemen, under the auspices of Williams College ·and the Smithsonian Institute, for the purpose of exploring parts of South America, and ot gathering treasures of Science and Art for the Institutions they represented.

On the tenth of October, the hearts of his kindred and numerous friends were overwhelmed with the tidings of his death, at Quito, on the fifth of September.

The resident members of the Council of the University, responding to the wishes of the whole community, appointed public religious services for the twenty-fourth of October, at which his sorrowing friends might give expression to their grief, and mingle their tears for a great and deeply felt bereavement.

Such services, commemorative of the life and character of the deceased, were held at the Presbyterian Church, in Le Roy. They were presided over by Chancellor Burchard, and participated in by the Board of Councilors, by the Faculty and Students of the University, and by a crowded congregation of sympathizing friends from the village and from abroad. On the wall, in the rear of the pulpit, was suspended a portrait of the deceased, by his own hand, surrounded by the symbols of his character and the beautiful drapery placed there by his afflicted neighbors and friends.

This small volume, in the main, is made up of the Addresses which were delivered on that occasion. It is published, especially, for circulation among personal and loving friends. ·Affection spontaneously insists upon placing these memorials together in a permanent form, as a grateful tribute to the conscious worth of the departed. Although no language can speak as did his beautiful life and presence, yet his portraiture, as here drawn, will be highly valued by his personal friends, and especially by the pupils of the Institution during his connection with it for the last twenty years.

The memory of a noble and stainless example is one of the most conservative and elevating forces of society. It is like the dew and the sunshine upon the hearts of men. It has a molding influence over mind and character, especially with the young and impressible, which works silently and powerfully, like nature's unseen forces, for the development and the triumph of the good and the excellent in mankind. This fact, doubtless, justifies the wide dissemination, by the press, of the memoirs of good and true men. And much more does it justify personal friends in gathering up the elements of excellence in their loved ones departed,— that their characters and their influence may live as a blessing to others, and especially, as a precious stimulus to themselves in toiling to complete successfully their own unfinished work.

INGHAM UNIVERSITY,
Le Roy, November, 1867.

BIOGRAPHICAL SKETCH.

BY REV. WM. L. PARSONS, D. D.

Col. PHINEAS STAUNTON died at the city of Quito, Ecuador, South America, Sept. 5, 1867, within eighteen days of his fiftieth birth day.

He was the son of Major-General Phineas, and Mrs. Mary Staunton, early settlers of Wyoming, in this State. General Staunton was a prominent officer in the war of 1812, was an intimate friend of General Peter B. Porter, the author, in Congress, of the war measure against England, and, with him, was intimately identified with the early progress of Western New York. The parents of Col. STAUNTON, judged by all that is now known of them, and by the revelation he has given of them upon the canvas, were persons of royal natures and of commanding characters.

As, in this case, it was emphatically true that the child was father of the man, let us look at our deceased friend in his boyhood, among the hills and valleys of Wyoming.

The lad is noted by all the neighbors, old and young, as promising a noble manhood. He is quiet, thoughtful, affectionate. He is diffident and retiring, and appears in society only when urged to do so, and, then, under the protest of a continually blushing face. A large soul shines out in all his little acts, and the neighbors ask him to

repeat his errands, that they may, a second time, enjoy the
glimmer from within. The physician is arrested, in his
practice, by an inexpressible something in that eloquent
eye which makes him wonder and admire. Of a quick
nature, the boy is precipitated into a passion under provo-
cation; but a word from an affectionate sister, reproving his
fault, melts his young heart, and his tears wash away his
offence. He is guileless, and his youth is believed not to
have been stained with an untruth. A mean thing he
cannot bear; and so, on one occasion, he falls to castigating
a neighboring boy, for which his mother, in turn, punishes
him. But inquiring, afterwards, why he did it, he replies:
" Mother, the boy treated his sister shamefully, and I could
not and I would not stand it." He is the model pupil in
the school, universally loved by teachers and scholars. He
carries in his manner the dignity and thoughtfulness of
manhood, and even the hired men so venerate the youth
that they will no more speak rudely to him than to his
father.

In his early boyhood, the elements of the future Artist are
stirring within him. As he goes forth to his toil in the
morning, he runs to the hill-top and fills his soul with the
beauties of the landscape,—occupies leisure hours in copying the pictures on the walls and making rude sketches
from nature. And later, when he has learned to handle the
brush, he shuts himself up alone and gives play to his passion. If, at any time, his powers will not work to his satis-
faction, he takes his flute, and, retiring to the river bank,
with sweet harmonies, persuades the muses to help him
adjust the currents of his nature to the enchanting work
before him. Visions of travel throng his young brain, and

he declares to his most intimate sister that he must see the world and sketch some of its most beautiful scenery; and, with this end in view, he, thus early, sets himself at the study of the languages of Europe.

Distinguished visitors, from far away, are at the family mansion; and the fame of the young man is borne beyond the Alleghanies among a people whom he afterwards visited, and who have since cherished his portrait almost as a sacred thing.

As he advances towards manhood, the spirit of self-dependence characterizes him. His own hands shall supply his wants or they shall go unsupplied; he will not burden his father, but will help him if he can. At eighteen years of age, he goes South to practice his art, having yet received no instruction himself, and, after one year, he returns bringing his sheaves with him, fourteen hundred dollars, which he is glad to place in the hands of his father.

Can we penetrate the inner being of this remarkable youth, and learn something of that mind, which is, already so beautifully revealing itself in the world?

Minds, like material organizations, have not all the same quality; they differ in their texture and substance. One is exquisitely delicate and highly wrought; another is coarse in its very grain and finish. Passing from the substance to the powers of the mind, the same law prevails. They are not alike in their measure, in their combinations, or in their adjustments. The intellects of some predominate largely over all the other powers. They run up like the lofty peaks of the mountains and penetrate the skies of thought; and they are as sharp, and clear, and imposing, and, often, as cold as they. The mind-world has its mountains, snow-capped and flame-lighted.

2

The emotional powers in other persons out-measure all the rest. Their sensibilities, like the ocean, are stirred by every motion of the elements,—by the impressions upon the senses and by the judgments of the reason, indiscriminately: and they are often as fickle as the sea.

Again, the will looms up high above all the other faculties, and makes some men embodiments of power. Natural laws, on a finite scale, seem incarnated in them. They are the engines of society. If their power were always directed by intelligent benevolence, they would be the world's greatest benefactors; but, lacking such direction, they often sweep through society like the tornado and uproot its most vital interests.

There are often seeming misadjustments, moreover, between the body and the mind. The mechanism of the two does not match. A too sanguine and nervous temperament involves grievous irritation, or a melancholic and bilious one takes the very light from the soul and imprisons it in darkness and semi-despair.

The religious nature, too, is not always proportionally developed. In some, it is weak and easily overborne; in others, it becomes a blind passion, inscribing altars "to the unknown God," and pushing the mind forward into intense devotion to mere forms and ceremonies of worship. In many, it is good to think, it awakens a conscious alliance with God, while dwelling among men; bears the thoughts up to communion with the Infinite and Perfect One, while we are physically confined to the finite and imperfect; and lays open to us our immortality, while we recognize the grave as our earthly goal.

And thus we have the general result, that very many

minds lack balance, symmetry, completeness. It is given but to few, to inherit such a mental constitution and such physical adjustments from the generations of the past, swept by the withering influences of sin and disease, that reason can hold her sceptre over all the mental and bodily powers, and shape the character according to the divine ideals which God has enstamped upon that highest function of our nature. Diseased appetites, disordered susceptibilities, lawless passions and prejudices, and falsehood baptized with the name of truth, are, in our world, sadly dominant over man's better nature.

I think all who knew Col. STAUNTON will concur with me in saying that he was, in a most remarkable degree, a happily constituted man. There was a surpassing refinement in his very nature, independently of any conscious expressions of it in his outward life. There was superiority in the very material of the man. The adjustments of his whole being were harmonious, beautiful. There was no disproportion which would strike one offensively or even unpleasantly. There was a rare unity in the grouping of his powers, an obvious symmetry in his whole organization which it was instructive to behold and study.

His intellect was broad, strong, active, greedy of knowledge, clear, comprehensive, and discriminating. His sensibility was in delightful adjustment to his other powers. A great thought, in his mind, took fast hold upon his emotional nature, which, remarkably free from all dominion of mere sense, was beautifully responsive to whatever he knew to be true, beautiful, and good.

His will was not of the sort which answers yea, yea; nay, nay; but was positive and unflinching in its devotion to

duty.   It was neither of that brittle nor of that flexible material which easily gives way under the severer pressure of
moral obligation.   His will and conscience could not be
easily divorced from each other.

Then, his bodily powers seemed beautifully correlated to
those of his mind.   His temperament was sufficiently sanguine to quicken into vigorous activity all the forces of his
nature, and also sufficiently choleric to secure a sustained
activity of his impulses in a patient and vigorous prosecution to the end, of all his plans, whatever might stand in
the way.

His whole being, then, was beautifully balanced.   It was
harmonious, symmetrical.   His higher nature had its just
and fixed ascendency over the lower.   He was, indeed, char-
acterized by an unusual moral elevation.

Nature designed and fitted him for an Artist; and a great
and good Artist he was.   And yet, while it was true that all
the forces within him culminated in his profession, he was not
thereby disqualified, like many persons endowed with special
gifts, for the practical duties of life in other directions.
Completely enveloped in the holy flame of Art, he could yet
instantly drop his palette and grasp his sword, when liberty
was assaulted in his native land.   He could throw his whole
soul into the scale of politics, if it seemed to him that the
beam was likely to go down on the side of injustice and
oppression.   He could couple his energies to the demands
of the University with which he was connected, and serve
its interests with great effect.   He could leave his studio
and join the enterprises of his brethren in the church as
devotedly as the best.

His religious, equally with his æsthetic nature, was in

beautiful proportion to his whole being. With the aid of his artist eye, he saw the Creator everywhere in his works, and had little temptation to bow before the altar of an unknown God. His religion could not be a blind passion, nor could he conceive of God, or of heaven, or of religious ideas, under the forms suggested by a mere technical theology. To his mind, God's nature and kingdom, the truths and glories of his universe, were all lighted up with his pervading presence, and with living, infinite beauty. With such a mind, worship could not well be a mere observance of ceremonies; it would naturally be a genuine communion of soul with soul, of the man with his Maker.

I have, thus far, considered the deceased mainly as to his constitutional nature. It is another question, how he used this beautiful organization of forces with which his Maker had endowed him. Was his moral character, as seen in his own responsible acts, as beautiful and complete as his natural? Did he honor God and honor himself in his life among men, as God honored him in giving him such endowments? Here we must find the true measure of the man, as a moral being and as entitled, or otherwise, to the grateful remembrance of his fellow-men.

And in considering his moral character, I shall not attempt to make out that he was never overcome by temptation. He was a man, and had the frailties of our common humanity. He was a sensitive man, and responded quickly to the motives which were adapted to excite his mind. God knows whether his responses were always approved in heaven.

The more I have studied and known Col. STAUNTON, the more thoroughly have I been convinced, that nothing aroused his mind to such intense moral action as the invasion of his sense of right and justice. The boy was father of the man, and the blows he gave to the lad who had "shamefully treated his sister," were prophetic of the blows, the man, as a matter of moral right, would be ready to administer with his tongue, to those whom he deemed guilty of outraging the rights of their fellow-men. He had nothing of that ignoble, contemptible tameness of nature which could allow him to see great wrong done and yet manifest no righteous indignation on account of it. With his equal intensity of nature and of moral principle, he must, when he saw his country wronged and outraged, be fired with a glowing resentment.

Then, to his artist ken, the discriminations between the right and just on the one hand, and their detestable opposites on the other, were so broad and deep, so immeasurable and impassable, that he could not fail to see the difference and feel it. There are men who excuse their want of moral resentment against what appears to be wrong, on the ground that they cannot see just where to draw the line between good and evil. Col. STAUNTON could never plead such a weakness of his nature as an excuse for taking no positive part in the great world-struggle between right and wrong.

He was not governed by what might seem a sort of blind moral principle. He was in sympathy with the better elements he could discern in men, while, at the same time, he stood in the most positive antagonism to every thing in them which offended his sense of honor and rectitude. He possessed the double virtue of loving the good and hating the evil he saw in men. Narrower minds will love the good and overlook the evil, or hate the evil and overlook the good in their fellow-beings.

The elements of our friend's moral and religious character, especially, were not open to universal inspection. He made no effort to display either his natural or moral qualities. He was retiring, and mingled little with men, rarely taking a conspicuous part in public assemblies. His devotion to his profession kept him mainly in his studio, and held him in close communion with objects which belong to the world of nature and of art. His life was on a higher plane than appertains to less gifted minds. Still, if we can occupy the right stand-point, it is not difficult to trace the elements of his religious nature as they manifested themselves in his Christian life and character.

What then was the inner law, the subjective purpose and end, upon which, as a living principle, his higher moral life was organized, and around which all his acts and energies centered themselves?

Col. STAUNTON's Christian life, as such, began at Wyoming, during one of those Pentecostal seasons so refreshing to the souls of men, when he was but eleven years of age. Some months later, when the fruits of the revival had been tested by the scorching sun and the piercing thorns of temptation, the inquiry arose among a gathered company of young converts, whether they were all honoring their new Master, and who was doing it most worthily. By common consent, they agreed that young PHINEAS STAUNTON was living the most consistent Christian life of them all.

And now, if we run our eye along the subsequent lines of his life, I think we shall find the true Christian spirit vigorously and victoriously asserting itself as entirely supreme in his soul.

Those noble and beautiful instincts which belonged, so

obviously, to his constitution, became, by his conscious choice, so incorporated into his moral life, that, thenceforth, they were to him among his fixed Christian principles. The remarkable purity of his nature became a conspicuous quality of his Christian character. No trait was more deeply impressive to those who knew him, than his pure-mindedness. His whole being heeded the injunction of Paul to young Timothy: "Keep thyself pure;" and to think on whatsoever things were pure, and true, and honest, and just, and lovely, was his delight.

While still a young man, at the age when the human heart is most easily assailed by the temptation to popular vices, he left his home and went far south, unavoidably exposed to these vicious habits; yet into no one of them did he fall. No profane word, no intoxicating drink, no narcotic stimulant, no vulgar language, ever defiled his lips.

Certainly, he was not engulfed in the absorbing passion for wealth which corrupts and ruins so many who attempt the Christian life. His passion was in the direction of Art, not of money. He entered most heartily, with Mrs. Staunton and her sister, into the purpose of making their earthly substance, with all their attainments, tributary to the cause of Christian education in their beloved University. The spare income from his profession was cheerfully laid upon that altar. He sacrificed distinction and wealth, as an Artist, for the good of Ingham University. A leading and controlling motive in joining the Scientific Expedition to South America, was that the cabinets of the Institution might be more completely and abundantly furnished for instruction in the Natural Sciences; so that his very life was laid down in the service of this school which his prayers had so often consecrated as a perpetual fountain of saving influences.

It was as a Christian patriot, apprehending the significance of the terrible assault upon the liberties of mankind, that Col. STAUNTON voluntarily engaged in the military service of his country. He hears the voice of God sounding through his studio, calling for the defense of human rights. He cannot rest, he cannot paint; the brushes drop from his fingers. He lays himself upon the altar of God and of his country, and, hastening to the fore-front of the battle, leads his men forward in the thickest of the fight. And, on the tented field, as at home, he is still the consistent, outspoken Christian. When the regiment is without a chaplain, he volunteers to serve in that capacity; and he does it to the edification and pleasure of all, for his exhortations and supplications come welling up from an earnest love of God and of man.

And, in that higher plane of his life, where, as an Artist, we see him surrounded by forms and visions of wondrous beauty, we are still impressed with the fact that his whole being is anointed with the unction that is from above, that the divine afflatus is lighting up and quickening the deepest impulses of his being. The Artist must, in the nature of things, be swayed by the ideals of his reason. He scarcely dwells in the world of sense or in the region of the logical understanding. The vital, quickening, transporting archetypes which God has stamped upon the higher spiritual nature—these furnish the Artist's inspiration. But the scale of these ideals starts in the finite and runs up into the infinite,—up to God himself; and the moral measure of the Artist is to be found in the particular ideals which absorb and

3

give direction to his genius. Is it an ideal human face, landscape, mountain, sea, or other sensible object which the Artist attempts to realize? Is it some finite thought, some historic story, some specimen of a generous, noble, or kingly man which he seeks to express upon the canvas?—then is he indeed an Artist, but not of the highest order. Run up the scale and find the man who is seeking to reveal, in beautiful forms, the character and thoughts of God himself, to put upon his canvas the breathings of the Holy One, to express to men the ideals of infinite, imperishable truth, beauty, and goodness, and you have the highest style of an Artist,—one whose life must needs be a Christian life, of the truest, purest, most elevated kind.

Col. STAUNTON, though interested in idealizing and expressing the characters and features of his friends upon the canvas, was also an Artist of this higher type. Personally attached to Henry Clay, he has, in the judgment of Mr. Clay's own sons, preserved for posterity the truest as well as the best ideal representation of that great patriot. Two portraits of him,—one in the Mayor's office, in the city of Brooklyn, and the other now at the University of Kentucky at Ashland, will forever attest the genius of our departed friend in this direction.

But we are looking for the Christian in the Artist, and we must go higher. And here, we find the truth to be, that all the compositions upon which Col. STAUNTON concentrated most earnestly the life forces within him, are eminently Christian. They are embodiments of the highest revealed thoughts of God, expressions of the highest conceptions of Christian feeling and faith. In his picture of *Lot's Escape from Sodom*, the Scripture scene glows upon the canvas;

in the *Walk to Emmaus*, how the coloring lights up the instructions which Jesus is giving to his disconsolate disciples. And on that canvas where Christ meets the man coming out from the tombs, exceeding fierce, how does Deity shine forth! And in his master-piece of *The Ascension*, what worlds of Christian thought and feeling has he expressed. There it stands, preaching to us of the risen Christ, with an eloquence which no living voice can command. And the highest study, the realization which, more than everything else he wished to reach, and on which, perhaps, years of thought had been spent, was a head of Christ himself, which should express, far more perfectly than any he had ever seen in this or other lands, the feeling of the Son of God in bearing the sins of the world. But this was an unfinished study which could only be completed in that higher studio to which he has ascended.

And now, on the principle that the man is greater than his works, I must conclude that Col. STAUNTON's faith in Jesus Christ was richer and better than anything he has been able to express of that saving grace ; that his Christian love transcended anything which he has ever made to glow upon the canvas. His nature was more beautiful than all the beautiful works he has left behind ; more noble than all the noble deeds he performed, for it produced them.

With his superior natural endowments,—with a taste so refined and universal, with his spontaneous repugnance to everything offensive to purity and truth, with his hearty relish for everything that was worthy of him, as a man, and with all his inflexible moral and religious principle, it was a matter of course, that he should be, as he was, the eminent and admired citizen, the noble man among men, the true friend, the practical and sincere Christian, the devoted husband, and affectionate father; and that he should richly adorn any sphere in which he might be called to move among men.

But time forbids me to linger. I have thus given, very imperfectly, my conception of our much loved brother and friend. To those who knew him intimately, and saw his life at its sources, it will seem far short of the reality. To those who knew him at all, I think it will appear only just.

The fact of the all-pervading grief of the community and the intense sympathy of friends far and near; that strong men and women gave themselves up to tears, when these sad tidings came; that their hands faltered in the labors of the day; that their heads reposed on sleepless pillows at night; that the very children, with tearful eyes, wondered why God did not have the bad men die and let the good ones live; that this throng of friends and neighbors have crowded this house to express their grief; and that these Christian friends have draped in mourning this Sanctuary of God, and placed about his suspended portrait, so touchingly, the symbols of the varied character of their friend and brother;—these facts pronounce a more fitting and expressive eulogy than any one man's pen can draw, and will more than justify all that I have ventured to say.

But the Lord has called his servant hence, while far, far from home, on foreign shores.

If Col. Staunton had been God's gift to his family and friends alone, it would seem fitting that he should have died at his cottage home, in Le Roy, with his dearest friends around him, ministering to his wants and sharing his sufferings.

If the ball which struck him at the head of his regiment, at Fair Oaks, had been a trifle less spent than it was, so that there he had fallen, to be buried on the bloody field " with his martial cloak around him," this would have seemed a fitting death for the noble, self-sacrificing Christian patriot. But no, God did not so appoint.

A few months ago, his early visions of travel dawned anew upon him; and, with buoyant hopes, palette and pencils in hand, he went forth, a member of a Scientific Expedition, organized at Williams College, and having the co-operation of the Government, to explore certain portions of South America; to climb its magnificent mountains, to look upon its wondrous scenery, to descend its great river, and to bring home large trophies for his studio and for the Halls of the University.

He had crossed the Isthmus, exploring Panama for a few hours, as being the stronghold where Pizarro stored his riches from Peru and expended millions upon his churches and theatres; then had sailed down the coast three hundred miles below Guayaquil to a small town in Peru, and back again to that seaport. There, some time was spent in exploring the region round about and in gathering interesting specimens. While at this point, the clouds lifted themselves from the hoary head of old Chimborazo, and he " saw it in the rosy light of morning," for once; " but that would do," he wrote, " for a life time." Here, sickness overtook the party, and four of them were detained for some days; but seeming measurably well again, their effects were packed upon mules, for the journey, up the mountains two hundred miles to the city of Quito. That city, just under the Equator, yet occupying one of the highest inhabited points on the globe, some ten to twelve thousand feet above the level of the sea, and enjoying a temperature of eternal spring, forms the center of one of the finest landscapes in the world. Eight snowy peaks of the Andes skirt the horizon and look down upon the city, with its 80,000 inhabitants, and upon the broad and beautiful plains of Anaquito and Turubamba, celebrated in the wars of Pizarro.

Starting towards this point from Guayaquil, all the artist fire was burning in the great soul of our brother. The goal of his earthly professional ambition was just before him. He had visited the renowned galleries of the old world and seen the works of the great masters. Now he was going up, two hundred miles into the gallery of the Almighty, to behold and wonder at the works of the Infinite Master. The vision grew richer, and broader, and grander, as he was borne upward. The panorama filled his great nature with sublimest emotions. He was almost face to face with God, the Maker of all. Borne on the shoulders of four men, weak, exhausted, but sustained, says Prof. Orton, by the magnificent scenery all around him, he entered Quito. Should he stop there? No. A Voice from above the mountains falls upon his ear, saying: " My child, come up higher—up higher—higher!" He obeyed the Voice, and went up higher,—up above all the mountains, among the visions of infinite beauty, perfection, and glory!

Was not that a fitting death for God to give to his artist child, whose mind, for half a century, had been reaching after those ideals which could be realized alone upon the hill-tops of the New Jerusalem?

There is still another item, harmonizing with all the rest, which should come into view, and which seems like the

certificate of the Father's loving care for both the departed
and those remaining. For hundreds of years, no Protestant
has been allowed Christian burial in the city of Quito; but,
through the agency of our beloved Government, whose life
our brother's sword had helped to defend, and just in time
for the sacred deposit, a Protestant cemetery had been pro-
cured "wherein never yet man was laid;" and by his, the
first burial therein, it was consecrated and set apart for the
Christian and peaceful interment of Protestant foreigners
who might lose their lives in that land of Papal idolatry.
These fitting words were spoken at the grave by Prof.
Orton, of the Expedition:

"Here stand the living,—no, the dying, burying the
dead. The seeds of dissolution are in us all: we must all
die; we are only travelers here, journeying on, as we trust,
to a better land. We express, in our mode of burial, our
faith: we believe in the Resurrection,—that, by some Almighty power and in some unknown way, these corruptible
bodies will take a celestial form. The very word we use
for this burial place,—cemetery,—meaning sleeping place, is
an expression of our belief that we shall rise again. Fellow
citizens, this is an unusual occasion. Yonder city of Quito
has stood for three hundred years, yet never has seen such
a day as this—the burial of a Protestant in a Protestant
burial ground. Through the efforts of our distinguished
representative, now numbered with the lamented dead, a
place has been allotted by this government, for the interment
of foreigners who unfortunately die in this country. This
day we consecrate it. It is fitting that the act of consecration should be done by the burial of a citizen of the great
Republic of the North. It is meet that the first one buried

here should be an officer in our second war of Independence, one of the brave men who led our armies in the defence of civil rights. It is proper that the first one buried here should be a member of a Scientific Expedition— the first one from the United States to Ecuador, regularly organized and recognized by our Government. We call this a Protestant cemetery, but not in a sectarian sense. We protest, in naming it thus, against the injustice and unchristian spirit which has existed so many years, of denying a decent burial to one who failed to agree with the national creed. Here may lie any one who believes in God. And, now, we bury our friend—his body, not his spirit, nor his memory. We commit this body to its kindred elements, earth to earth, dust to dust, waiting in faith for the morning of the Resurrection, when earth and sea shall give up their dead. And may the blessing of Him who is the Resurrection and the Life, abide with us forever,— Amen."

And were we standing at the center of that far off cemetery to-day, we should, with tearful emotions, read on a new tablet this inscription :

TO THE MEMORY OF

Col. PHINEAS STAUNTON, A. M.,

VICE CHANCELLOR OF INGHAM UNIVERSITY, LE ROY, N. Y., U. S. A.,

And Member of the Scientific Expedition from

WILLIAMS COLLEGE and SMITHSONIAN INSTITUTE,

WHO

Died, September 5th, 1867, Aged 50 Years.

Requiescat in pace.

And now, to the dear ones gazing up into heaven after the beloved, vanished form, what saith the Voice which called him to his heavenly home? As I stand before the great picture of *The Ascension* of our now undying Artist, with a listening soul, I seem to hear that same Voice from above, bidding us return to the Jerusalem of our earthly labors; thence to go forth, with an unwonted baptism, to testify the grace of God, and to finish the work he has given us to do, until the day come when, in the cloud of glory, we too, shall ascend into His Holy Presence.

ADDRESS BY CHANCELLOR BURCHARD.

I need not add a word to the just, appropriate, and beautiful tribute, to which you have just listened. We are mourners, and need comfort. A heavy blow has fallen upon our hearts, and we feel the severity of the stroke. The widow bereaved mourns the loss of a devoted and loving companion, who with her was identified in all her sympathies and pursuits. This church mourns the loss of one of her most intelligent and efficient members—an elder, greatly appreciated and beloved, and these symbols of sadness show the estimate in which he was held. The University, with which he had been so long connected as Vice Chancellor, feels the loss, and its numerous pupils, here and elsewhere, realize that a father and friend has fallen. This whole community, indeed, experiences to-day one common sentiment of grief, and we all—widow, sister, brother, kindred, and friends—meet and mingle in these memorial exercises with hearts stricken and sad, and what we need is comfort, solace, in this deep and unexpected bereavement. It is pleasant that we are able to refresh our minds by memories of departed worth, to recall a life devoted to the noblest pursuits, a heart freighted with all that was generous and good, a genius that had wrought and won unfading laurels. The letters from friends, so full of tenderness and sympathy, have come as balm to the wounded heart. Still, in the midst of broken hearts and hopes, we must look higher for the needed support in this hour of trial. "God alone is our refuge and strength, a very present help in trouble." Let us apply the elements of comfort as gathered from his blessed Word.

Is it not, then, as we feel the pressure and severity of the blow, a comfort to realize and know that God has inflicted it? No enemy, no accident, as a cause, has been at work in this series of events which has terminated in the removal of our beloved friend. The time of his death, the place. the circumstances, the burial in a strange land, were all arranged in the Divine Mind, were in the plan and purpose of God. "Is there evil in the city; is there sorrow upon our hearts; has calamity fallen suddenly upon us, and the Lord hath not done it?" Surely there is comfort and strength in the thought, that all things, all events, whether prosperous or adverse, are under the direction and control of the ever blessed God, "who ordereth all things after the counsel of his own will, and there is none that can stay his hand or say, what doest thou?" When the pious Eli received the revelation of judgment, that was to come upon his household, he was calm, and said: "It is the Lord; let him do what seemeth him good." When the hope of the Psalmist was prostrate, recognizing the Divine hand in the bereavement, he said: "I was dumb; I opened not my mouth because *Thou* didst it!" But when we are afflicted, how much richer the consolation to know that he afflicts for good, that it is a part of his plan to discipline and prepare the soul for his own glorious presence in heaven. "Though no chastisement for the present seemeth to be joyous but grievous; yet, nevertheless afterward it yieldeth the peaceable fruits of righteousness to them that are exer-

cised thereby." Chastisement, trial of any kind, is sad. It
was designed to be so. It exercises the soul with grief. If
it did not, it would be no chastisement, and would fail to
realize "the peaceable fruits of righteousness." "Whom the
Lord loveth he chasteneth, and scourgeth every son whom
he receiveth." Let us then welcome trial as a token of
affection—as an evidence of sonship; "knowing that our
light affliction, which is but for a moment, worketh for us a
far more exceeding and eternal weight of glory." Is it not
enough for us to know, when calamity comes, when riches
take to themselves wings, when friends sicken and die,
when the shadows deepen, that "all things work together
for good to them that love God?" "I can endure the fires
of the furnace, if I am assured that only the dross is to be
consumed: I can endure chastisement, if chastisement is to
pass into discipline; discipline, into piety; and piety, into
heaven." Such is the divine plan and process. "It is
through much tribulation, that we are to enter into the
kingdom." We should not seek exemption, we should
not desire to escape the sifting and the purifying process,
and especially when we are assured that grace shall be
equal to our day, that the divine strength shall be made
perfect in weakness. We may stand appalled in the presence of the great calamity that has fallen upon us; we may
wonder at this mystery of the Divine Providence; but in
the view taken of the purpose of God in affliction, may we
not hope that good will come from this loss? We may not
see it, but faith is assured of it. It may be too glorious for
us now to see, but it will come in its full fruition, and God's
goodness shall be so manifest that we shall wonder at the
wisdom of the way along which he hath led us. Let us wait

patiently, submissively, for the unfolding of the mystery. To him who sees as we can not, the mystery is already solved. The good which we anticipate, is realized to him. He has left us, it is true, and left us in sadness. He has left the field of his labors and successes; he has left the monuments of his genius behind him.

But what is this *leaving*, of which we speak? It is not death, nor annihilation, nor a cessation of consciousness, but an exit, a departure, a triumph. "Christ hath abolished death and brought life and immortality to light through the gospel." What are those sublime words that come sounding down through the ages like the voice of a clarion: "I am the resurrection and the life; he that believeth in me, though he *were* dead, yet shall he live: and whosoever liveth and believeth in me shall never die." Our departed friend was a Christian; he believed in Jesus. His life was hid with Christ in God, and he is not dead, but realizes life in its sublimest sense. "To be absent from the body is to be present with the Lord." And who of us, at times, has not sympathized with the Apostle in his heavenly vacillation, "I am in a strait betwixt two having a desire to depart and be with Christ, which is far better." This earthly life is sweet; it is good to be here beneath these calm skies, on this green earth. It is good to live in the confidence and affection of earthly friends, and to unite with them in labors of love; but it is better to depart and be with Christ. Our friend realizes this now as he never *did* and never *could* while here. He loved life; he loved the scenes of earth; he loved art and beauty; and it was his love for the grand and beautiful in nature that led him from his beautiful home to climb the heights of the Andes.

He was enamored by that strange and wonderful scenery. His soul was in an ecstasy of delight. But he sees stranger things now. All the wonderful panorama of God's wisdom and works is moving before him; and the Artist's taste and the Christian's hope are fully realized in that world of endless beauty and beatitude; and could he speak to us, he would say :—

"I shine in the light of God,
  His image stamps my brow,
Through the vale of death my feet have trod,
  And I reign in glory now.

"No breaking heart is here,
  No keen and thrilling pain,
No wasted check where the frequent tear
  Has rolled and left its stain.

"I have reached the joys of heaven,
  I am one of its sainted band,
To my head a crown of gold is given,
  And a harp is in my hand.

"I have learned the song they sing,
  Whom Jesus has set free,
And the glorious walls of Heaven still ring
  With my new-born melody.

"No sin, no grief, no pain ;
  Safe in my happy home,
My fears all fled, my doubts all slain,
  My hour of triumph's come.

"Oh! friends of mortal years,
  The trusted and the true,
Ye are waiting yet in the vale of tears,
  But I want to welcome you.

" Do I forget ?   Oh ! no—
    For memory's golden chain
  Still binds my heart to your hearts below,
    Till they meet and touch again.

" Each link is strong and bright,
    And love's electric chain
  Flows freely down, like a rill of light,
    To the world from whence it came. ,

" Do you mourn when another star
    Shines out in the glittering sky ?
  Do you weep when the raging voice of war
    And the storms of conflict die ?

"Then why do your tears run down,
    Why are your hearts so riven,
  For another gem in your Saviour's crown,
    And another soul in Heaven ?"

ADDRESS OF COUNCILOR REV. JOS. R. PAGE.

I have been requested to participate in these exercises, designed to honor the dead and to benefit the living. To do so is a labor of love. After what has been spoken in discriminating and truthful commendation of the departed; in the expression of the general and deep grief his decease has occasioned throughout the entire community, and our heart-felt and profound sympathy with the chief mourner :

> " When *such* friends part,
> 'Tis the survivor dies "—

it may seem unnecessary to add anything to what has already been so well said. But if I advance nothing new, I shall, at least, be an additional witness to the truth, and shall gratify my own heart in testifying to the exalted worth of our deceased friend and brother.

None could be acquainted with him without recognizing a character of rare Christian manliness, and prizing his friendship. I will venture to say, with all confidence, that no one was ever associated with him in the management of the Institution with which he was so long identified, as henceforth to be held in everlasting remembrance by its benefactors and friends, who did not learn to form and cherish a warm affection for him ; so gentle was he in spirit, so courteous in manner, so kind in speech, and yet so decided in his opinions, and firm in his advocacy of abstract

5

right above all mere expediency, and uniform exemplification of the sentiment. On the stock of an amiable, lovely disposition, there was grafted, by the Divine Spirit, a scion of the heavenly land, which gave to his life beauty, and fragrance, and fruitfulness. We weep to-day, because so much that was pleasant and good; that was blessed in itself and a blessing to others, has gone down to the grave.

Yet though we weep, we do not murmur. We do not forget whose work it is. Chance, accident, fatality, had nothing to do with it. *The hand of God was uplifted to lay our brother low.* Not in anger toward him, not in indifference to us, did the blow fall. No, no. God is as good now as he was before he took the departed to himself. We can not distrust his loving kindness. We have no reason to do so. Because he is incomprehensible in his ways, we rather learn to adore him. Our bleeding hearts cry out with one of old: "It is the Lord; let him do what seemeth him good,"—fully satisfied that nothing *seems* good to God that is not *really* so.

Nor are we disposed to indulge in vain regrets of that fatal journey to the southern hemisphere, and in restless speculations of what might otherwise have been. Enough for us to know it was deliberately chosen, carefully planned, entered upon with prayer, for commendable, noble purposes, and consecrated to the good of man and the glory of God. That it was not unattended with danger all knew, but none could foresee its end. It was the will of God that it should be made, and that it should result as it has. The divine plan provided for it, and like the accomplishment of all God's purposes by his creatures, of his own choice our brother carried it into execution. We need strong conso-

lation when such men suddenly die. And here, pre-emi-
nently, it is to be found; the eternal decrees of God contemplated it: his sovereignty determines the event, and
freely, in the exercise of his own volition, the subordinate
agent moves on to its accomplishment.

Blessed be God, the hand of the Lord shaped every inci-
dent in the last days of the departed. There was not one
bitter drop in the cup of which he drank, that his Heavenly
Father did not place there, according to his purpose, from
the beginning. So he received it, and when his prayer
ascended to the Mercy Seat, that if it were possible the cup
might pass from him, it ended with the words of Jesus:
" Nevertheless, not my will, but thine, be done." In the
exercise of this spirit, sustained by this faith, we cast our
burden on the Lord to-day.

For a moment, let us look Death in the face, to see what
he really is. Only to unbelief, is he now the King of
Terrors. Faith in Jesus transforms the "last enemy" into
a friend. The Captain of our Salvation has plucked out his
sting: has converted the dread monarch into a faithful ally
of his people. He did this by his own descent into the
grave, and his victory over its powers of darkness.

Chiefly did Christ come into the world *to die.* This was
his main design. We do not overlook his mission as the
Light of the world, the Great Teacher and Example of the
race; we do not forget this when we say: "The lamb slain
from the foundation of the world," became incarnate to
actualize this ideal, and receive the homage of the universe
forever, as " *The Lamb Slain.*" He won his triumph by his
death.

Why, then, should we regard the death of the righteous

as so great a calamity? Who can tell what seeds of good may be scattered by it?—what influences to bless the world may originate in it? Our deceased brother possessed so much of the self-sacrificing spirit of the Master, that he counted not his life dear, so that he might meet all his obligations, and accomplish, in the highest degree, the design of his being. In the hour of his country's peril, he hastened to the field of battle, there to die, if such was the will of God, for her salvation.

In the exercise of the same spirit, on a different field, he has fallen. And who doubts that it is better to die thus, than to live in mere selfish enjoyment of the good things of God?—that it is more noble to meet death in the effort to make the most of what we are and have, both for ourselves and others, than it is to live in sluggish ease, a stranger to the sublimest aspirations of the human soul!

Were mine the power to restore among us the manly form so dear, we shall never look upon on earth again; to call up from the grave the body sleeping its last sleep,—thank God! it is "A sleep in Jesus," on the far distant shores of the South Pacific, and bring him into these Courts of the Lord he so loved to frequent, and into this pulpit, and here break from his lips the seal of eternal silence death has placed thereon, we should hear him say: "Weep not that I shall return to you no more; I have met death where it was most fitting that I should, in the effort to make the most of life; most successfully to serve my generation and my God, and there I leave for your imitation an example of devotion to the great ends we were made to seek. Follow me, as I have followed Christ."

MEMORIAL LETTER OF A FORMER PASTOR.

MONROE, MICH., OCT. 17, 1867.

REV. W. L. PARSONS, D. D.

Dear Sir:—Your letter of the 12th inst, announcing the death of Col. PHINEAS STAUNTON, reached me last evening, just at the going down of the sun.

Not a shadow had pre-heralded the event. It was like rain falling from a clear blue sky, and yet it was like a bolt from a dark cloud to my soul. I did not, could not anticipate such an event. I knew where he was, but could only think of him in this new path of adventure, as adding brighter lustre to a name and a fame undying in the affections of all who knew him.

The friendship between Col. STAUNTON and myself, was formed in early manhood. It has grown and strengthened with the on-going of time. Nothing has ever impaired that friendship, and though death has placed the "dark valley" between us, I trust we shall meet again "on the other side," but to renew and perpetuate, eternally, what was begun in time.

Allow me to recall some of the more marked traits in the character of my departed friend—traits that endeared him to those who knew him most intimately. He was a man of warm and earnest affections, in the retired walks of the domestic and social relations. His profession secluded him in a great measure from the noise and glare of the outside world; and this may have left the impression on some minds, that there was about him, if not within him, a want of sympathy with his fellows. This was not so. Never did I know one whose soul was more completely devoted to the home of his childhood. Every path, nook, and dell, was as familiar to him as the outlines of a friend's face on the canvas in his studio. True, it was a spot to love, as from the hill-side, it looked forth upon the beautiful valley at its base,—colossal bluffs forming the background. He never tired of beholding or talking about these scenes. The name and deeds of his revered father, linked as they were with the stirring events of the war of 1812, seemed to be incorporated in his very being,—a part of his living self. His kindred loved him, and vied to do him honor. They felt, and all who knew him in the intimacies of real friendship felt, that they could trust him. Destitute of these qualities, no amount of genius or brilliancy of talents can give that fascination to the character that wins lasting affection.

It is not my intention to eulogize our departed friend, and brother. Were I to attempt the theme, in addition to the elements of a stern Christian integrity and humility, ever apparent, I should give a large space to that beautiful symmetry or harmony of parts, which gives the chiefest charm to a truly Christian, manly character. Courage and humility were beautifully blended in the life of our departed friend,—so modest and unpretending, he often kept silent when those with whom he mingled regretted that he did not speak; and yet, when stern duty called him to act, he promptly responded to the call. As a citizen, he was enterprising, entering with enthusiasm into all plans that were

·for the general good. He was an ardent lover of his country,—he loved her institutions of government, of learning, and religion. For her liberties, he was willing, when called, to buckle on the sword and die in their defense.

It may be, there are some obscuring partialities in my long and uninterrupted friendship with Col. STAUNTON. I cannot feel otherwise, than that I have lost one of my truest friends on earth. While I can think of him in no other light than as pleasant to all who knew him, I must be permitted to say, "Very pleasant hast thou been unto *me*." It is very sad to know that I shall never see that manly form, or gaze into that face, beaming with intelligence and kindness, any more. That body sleeps in an unknown grave. That lustrous eye is closed in death;—the voice is hushed in silence, and that good right hand that transferred to the canvas the communings of the soul with nature, and "nature's God," has lost its skill. He was an Artist from necessity, no less than choice. The God who made him, endowed him with a fine imagination, most exquisite taste, and admiration of the sublime and beautiful, whether in nature or art: and, with true devotion to his calling, he has given unwearied pains to the cultivation of all the nobler faculties of his being. He was an ornament to every circle in which he moved, and honored every trust committed to him. He will be missed from many a centre of usefulness and happiness on earth. The Church of Christ has lost an ardent friend;—the University has lost a firm pillar, in its Vice Chancellor and Secretary;—the Country has lost a Scholar, and true Patriot.

We would not invade the deep solemnities of the domestic sanctuary, but to say, there sits solitary and silent, one to whom "the dead" was more precious than to all others on earth.

Dear One:—Remember that *He*, who hath taken, "doeth all things well." His body sleeps in the grave, but we confidently believe his immortal part has gone to that heavenly land to which that eldest Sister so recently took her flight.

The Soldier has laid off his armor, and is now reposing amid the trophies of victory. The Artist has left his Studio of finished and unfinished pictures on earth, to enter into and forever gaze upon, and wonder at the seraphic forms and matchless glories of the "upper Temple."

I regret that I cannot be present in your memorial service, to mingle my voice, and tears, "with those that weep." Accept this poor tribute of one who will ever delight to honor the memory of the beloved STAUNTON.

Let our consolations come from Him, from whom all consolations flow.

"God is our refuge, and strength, a very present help in trouble; therefore will not we fear, though the earth be removed, and though the mountains be carried into the midst of the sea, though the waves thereof roar, and be troubled, though the mountains shake with the swelling thereof."

C. N. MATTOON.

FROM A LETTER OF D. R. BACON, ESQ.

It was my good fortune to know your dear departed husband well, during his many years of residence among us; and what a noble record that residence has made! As a patriot, a teacher, an artist, and, above all, as a christian, he has gone to his rest without a stain and without a reproach. It was those qualities, so nobly and so fully illustrated in the whole life of Col. STAUNTON, that rendered the announcement of his sudden death, in a distant land, so afflicting to this community, and, to a multitude of friends, gave it the force and shock of a personal bereavement.

It is with friends, as with blessings, that they are only justly prized when they take their departure. In the quiet, but earnest manner in which your cherished husband was devoted to the art which he had chosen, and which he adorned, it would not be likely that those manly and noble qualities of heart and soul which were conspicuous to those with whom he was more intimately associated, should be generally known and appreciated. But to those outside of this intimate circle, there was conspicuous in his life, a purity and consistency of character, a catholic and tolerant spirit, a sense of the full obligation of the citizen, unsullied by any selfish aim, and more than all, a genuine patriotism which all could see and admire, and which rendered his example as perfect as is often found among men. None in

6

this community can forget with what alacrity, in the hour
of our country's trial, he left his studio, regarding the call
as *personal,* and with what zeal and earnestness he labored
to inspire others with the same enthusiasm, until his regiment was raised, which he led in person to the post of
danger,—doing (as in everything) his duty bravely and
manfully in the enemy's front,—and only leaving when
pressing duties demanded his return.

But this is not the place or the occasion for his eulogium.
How much indeed might be said of him in any and every
department of duty which he has been called to fill. How
lovingly and carefully did he watch over and foster the
interests of the Institution with which he was, with your-
self, inseparably associated. How rapt was his soul in
devotion to his noble profession! How elevated were the
chosen subjects of his pencil, which was already winning
him a name for their originality, power, and vividness of
conception, and truth and beauty of execution.

It will never be permitted us to know how much is lost
to Art, by this premature death,—just at the hour when his
genius had been kindled by the surpassingly sublime and
beautiful scenes from the higher Andes. But the marked
feature which distinguished him as an Artist,—growth,—
leads all that knew him to believe that he would have
stepped upon a higher plane, and that his pencil would have
developed increased *breadth* and *power.* I trust that some
appreciative and capable hand will do him justice as an
Artist. Unskilled as I am, the qualities that struck me as
the most noticeable, and in which he would not suffer in
comparison with our most distinguished painters,—were
the admirable blending of light and shade, in which nature

was exactly transferred to canvas,—his natural groupings, in which the characters were marked, distinctive, and always in keeping and equal to our ideal; and all so subor-dinate to the main subject of his design, that when it left his hands there was a *completeness*, which, like a perfect poem, left little for the imagination to supply.

It is our country then, as well as this community and his nearer home circle, that should mourn .the loss of such a man.　He has gone, just as his advance was the most marked,—when his growth was well assured, and when his distinguishing merits and excellencies were certain to rank him among the very first in American Art.　But he "still lives," in the works he has left behind, not as a copyist, but as a bold, original, truthful delineator of those higher sub-jects which always inspired the genius of the Great Masters.

RESOLUTIONS.

The following Preamble and Resolutions were unanimously adopted by the Board of Councilors of the University, at a special meeting held on the 24th of October, 1867 :

Whereas,—Intelligence has been received of the decease of the honored and beloved Vice Chancellor of this Institution, Col. PHINEAS STAUNTON, A. M., in Quito, Ecuador, South America, Sept. 5, 1867, whither he had gone, with a company of scientific gentlemen, to gratify a thirst for knowledge, and the love of the wonderful and sublime in nature, chiefly to procure from that strange and peculiar land a valuable addition to the Cabinets of this Institution ; therefore,

1. *Resolved,*—That we deeply deplore the loss of one so admirably qualified for the prominent position he has held and honored in Ingham University since its incorporation, by natural endowment, careful and thorough culture, and the grace of God ; by the rare combination of many and striking excellencies, a child-like spirit, blended with manly vigor ;—uniformly genial, affable, and courteous, yet ever faithful to his convictions ; habitually manifesting both the interest and the purity of a father to all committed to his care ;—by eminence as an artist, and skill as an instructor : and that, mingled with our sense of this loss, is

the sore grief of parting with a highly prized and personal
friend, greatly endeared to each of us by all our intercourse
in the past, in every relation we sustained to each other,
especially as joint members of this Board.

2. *Resolved*,—That the Providence by which he was suddenly cut off, in the full vigor of his manhood, the
highest degree of his usefulness, and his greatest devotion
to the cause of education in general, and to this Institution
in particular, is to us altogether incomprehensible, and leads
us to adore the wisdom and goodness of God we cannot see,
but do not doubt were in exercise in his removal, and to
meekly bow in quiet submission to his sovereign, holy will.

3. *Resolved*,—That in the Expedition, which resulted in
his death, we recognize the same self-sacrificing spirit that
led him, in the hour of his country's peril, to enter the
army as a volunteer,—an act of Christian patriotism which
this Board cannot suffer to pass in silence, or to be named
but with the highest commendation.

4. *Resolved*,—That, as the " strong rod " and " beautiful
staff" of this Institution are thus broken, and cease to support and adorn it, we will confide more implicitly and
directly than ever in God, to establish and make it increase-
ingly and permanently a Power in the Land, to bless our
daughters and honor His name.

5. *Resolved*,—That, to perpetuate and honor the name of
the deceased in the annals of Ingham University, we will

take immediate measures to endow a professorship, to be called the "Staunton Professorship of the Fine Arts."*

6. *Resolved,*—That we hereby give expression to our tender and profound sympathy with the deeply bereaved widow of the deceased: mingling our tears with hers, we affectionately commend her to Him "who healeth the broken in heart and bindeth up their wounds," that He will comfort and sustain her in this double and speechless sorrow.

---

* In accordance with this vote, the Rev. Joseph R. Page, of Perry, N. Y., has been appointed Financial Secretary, to raise funds for the University. Any of the friends of Col. STAUNTON disposed to aid in the establishment of this professorship to his memory, can forward their contributions to him.

ADDRESS OF REV. S. MERRILL.

In the dim and silent hall of a ruined castle, the curious seeker found an ancient harp, perfect as when last played upon by human hands; but the music was hushed, and the minstrel was gone. So there is before us to-day a vacant seat,—yonder, the cottage home,—and there again, are the implements of an artist; but the citizen, the husband, the artist, has gone! The manly form,—the full, expressive eye, the pleasant accents of the voice—the thoughtful face, before which a vision of the highest ideal constantly passed— all, with the appointed pilgrimage, are ended, and we have paused, in the currents of our busy lives, to speak a word of comfort to the bereaved, a word of true praise for the departed, and to gather lessons for ourselves.

It is but a few weeks since Col. STAUNTON worshiped with us in this house of God. To-day he is sleeping in a new-made grave, amid the lofty mountains of a distant country. Setting out on a mission of which we anticipated with pleasure the grand results,—the ocean and its winds proved his friends, and bore him safely to the place of his destination. But unlooked for messengers were waiting his arrival; and when they called, our friend, surrounded by the emblems of a false religion, and the accents of a strange people, cheerfully yielded up his life.

By this providence of God, we must solemnize to-day an empty funeral! But by His grace, these services shall be

7

no empty memorials,—but as warm and rich as sympathy and esteem can make them.

A great multitude is gathered within these sacred walls, but in spirit we are far away beneath the burning Equator, among the snowy peaks of the Andes, standing, with heads uncovered and faces bowed, about a lonely grave, while, with trembling utterance, our hearts express a deep and common sorrow.

Memorials of an Artist! When was such another scene witnessed in Le Roy? How can we help weeping over a loss which cannot be repaired? We respect and honor those gifted intellects whose volumes are our study and delight. We admire that genius which smoothes for us the paths of science, and opens to us the fair temple of knowledge. But it is a higher admiration and a richer praise which we bestow upon the Christian Artist, inasmuch as he brings to us the choicer treasures. Passing beyond the sphere of ordinary comprehension, he hears the music of the storm; he sees the beauty in earth and sky; he feels the currents of a higher life; he catches the delicate realities of the inner life of man; he reveals those rich and harmonious blendings of the finite with the infinite; and when, by silent, patient study and toil, he has placed these noble truths upon the canvas, he has given to his fellow-men that which will elevate and purify the soul. It was in this way, that our departed friend had enviable success in bene-fitting others.

Of the many excellent qualities which commend him to us as a worthy example, I need not speak further, because they have been so well developed and set forth in the narra-tive which we have just heard from Dr. Parsons. The purity of his thought and intention; his constant appeal, whenever he spoke, to good feeling and good sense: his uniform kindness, courtesy and affection; his cheerfulness, even when suffering from weariness or pain: the charm of his hopeful spirit: the quietness of his numerous deeds of charity: his loyalty to his country; his boldness for the truth: his humility as a Christian,—these, as well as zeal, patience, punctuality, and a large public spirit, are among the virtues which were prominent in the character of our friend, and which it would be wise in us to imitate.

In addition to these traits, there is one feature of his character which has not been mentioned, and which commends itself to our notice, by its rarity, as well as by its prominence in him. I refer to his constant desire and effort to do his best. Always to do one's best is commendable in any person. But in the life of our friend, this rule had the widest possible meaning. It was not limited to doing the best for his own interests, or the best under any given circumstances: but he aimed to do the very best for others. Hence he was willing to risk his life in the burning and poisoned tropics, that he might bring back some gathered treasures for the University. If he painted a portrait, he sought to express the features of the soul, as well as of the face. When he seeks to call back to the living canvas the master spirit of Kentucky, the most intimate friends of the great orator declare that the work is unsurpassed. When the dream of his early days comes true, and he sails to visit the wonders of the old world, instead of passing to Italy that he might tread its enchanted soil, and be inspired by its ages of literature, and art, and song, he stops in Paris and toils for weeks and months in

copying from the great masters of his art those pictures
which should adorn the halls of learning at his own home.
And again, in that fearful hour, when, leading his men in
battle, or marching upon some blazing battery, the thought
uppermost in his mind was how he could use his strength
and skill, or give his life if necessary, for his imperiled
country. And this noble ambition, of doing the very best
for others, regardless of the consequences to himself, followed him through all his successful career. And even
now, if it were in his power—not for his own interest, but
for the wishes and happiness of others—he would give back
his dead body to his friends and fellow-citizens who mourn
his departure.

He was eminently a Christian Artist. Christ had sub-
dued his soul and re-modeled his ideals. Because of this
in-dwelling spirit, he was a good steward of the excellent
gifts which he had received of God. Because of this spirit,
an influence goes out from his life as pure as the light, as
gentle as the dew. Because of it, there is a sweetness
about his memory which will never pass away. In him,
ambition, and genius were still farther refined and sancti-
fied by the presence of the in-dwelling Christ. It is chiefly
for this reason, that his example gives a lofty meaning to
life, a rich beauty to the doctrines of the gospel, a charm to
every social virtue, and an emphasis to the joys of home,
and kindred, and friends.

This great and good man has passed away!

God is building a temple, and He gathers for it the
choicest materials,—the most precious stones, the stalwart
oak, and the stately palm, the fairest flowers, and the most
lovely forms,—things which are needed on earth, but are

needed more in heaven. Oh, the royal honor of being " builded together " for that " holy temple !"

Our friend has passed from labor to rest. From a land of perpetual summer, he passed to the Paradise above. From the perfumed breezes of the tropics, to the balmy airs of heaven. Sleep, O brother, in your far-off mountain grave ! Christ, who is the resurrection and the life, will not forget your resting place !

Allston, one of the finest of Christian artists, left incomplete, at his death, a picture which had been the study of his life. The same was true of Titian. The same is true also in the case of our departed friend. A pupil of Titian sought to complete the unfinished picture of his master. Who will dare take up the unfinished work of STAUNTON ? Oh, if he could come back to us ! how would he trace, with angelic skill, the face of the Saviour, and reveal unto us the glories of *The Ascension.*

But it is difficult for the intellect to make its way when the heart demands to be heard. Sympathy is better than praise. If I could impart unto you the sympathy of Christ, I should do a greater service to your bleeding hearts than the offering of any eulogy.

Friends of the departed ! we offer you this mournful tribute of farewell !

My Christian Sister, upon whose heart the heaviest blow has fallen, the depth of your sorrow cannot be measured by words. For you, the silver cord is loosed,—the golden bowl in which your earthly joys and hopes were gathered, is dashed in pieces. I can assure you that, out of this trial, there will come a new charm in bearing the cross, a new sweetness in the Saviour's love, and a richer meaning to the word *rejoice!*

Well, bereaved one! the hour cometh quickly when the "narrow sea" will cease to divide you from your husband. He is in glory. You yet remain in this shadowy land,—a shadowy land, yet for you, so full of stern realities, of toil, and of hope, of struggle and of prayer.

But there is One who watches above you, and who will sustain you till the last. He, who hath been the dwelling place of His people in all generations—the slightest whisper of whose infinite spirit is sweeter to the stricken soul than the music of silver bells,—He will be your refuge in this distress;—His hand shall wipe away all tears from your eyes; His voice shall soothe your soul in this deepest sorrow; His divine sympathy shall gather about you like the folds of a spotless raiment. The angel of his presence shall come to you in your loneliness and be better to you than any earthly friend; and when, at last, His voice shall welcome you, as it has welcomed your companion,—from labor to rest,—your sorrow and toil shall then be swallowed up in victory and joy.

COL. STAUNTON, AS AN ARTIST.

Some features of Col. STAUNTON's character, as an Artist, were rare singleness of aim; capacity for earnest, thorough work; the love of Art for its own sake; a large reserve of available power, ensuring growth; and, above all, an obvious genius for idealizing the forms of nature and expressing the thought which they embody.

With these characteristic qualities, he had already achieved a considerable amount of valuable work, which his modesty alone withheld from fame; while his freshness of nature, and his habits of patient toil, gave assurance of continued progress and increasingly excellent results. His original and striking conceptions, power of expression, and effective manner, all indicated great possibilities, which time was certain to develop. He wrought slowly, but was sure of every step. In his finished pictures, there is no trace of weakness or indecision, of fatigue or haste,—no faltering in his high purpose, or in his assured confidence of success.

There was one marked feature of Col. STAUNTON, as a man, which had much to do with his character as an Artist. To his mind, a true and noble life far transcended the most perfect creations of Art. This was his highest ideal, the realization of which was the first purpose of his soul. Believing that genius is dependent, for its best development, upon purity and simplicity of character, he aimed to make his life a living picture of all sweet and noble traits, and all

useful activities. He painted, indeed, a less amount of
canvas, but he infused into all his work a truer soul, a
larger element of the divine. With his eye ever lifted
toward the vision vouchsafed from heaven, he could not
paint otherwise than conscientiously, and, in a sense, relig-
iously : could not, at the bidding of a lower nature, paint
merely for applause, or fame, or money. He had the power
of genius, to elevate and spiritualize, without destroying
resemblances ; and he could not satisfy himself without
expressing, on the canvas, more than mere outward likeness.
His portraits, therefore, if they sometimes seemed unsatisfactory at first, were sure to " improve upon acquaintance."

The subjects of Col. STAUNTON's paintings had all the
variety which marked his characteristics as a man. His
first years were devoted mostly to landscapes and to portraits ;—though one of his most careful early studies was
prophetic of the tendencies of his maturer genius. This
was *The Risen Christ*, as, in the garden, he said to Mary,
"Touch me not, for I am not yet ascended." In his gallery
of later productions, we see hardly any one style predomi-
nant; but, in almost equal excellence, portraits, real and
ideal ;—of childhood, of manhood, and of womanhood, in
their purest, noblest types—landscapes, historical, and scrip-
tural scenes ; and to the last, he was increasingly devoted.
Henry Clay, a portrait from life, in the City Hall, Brooklyn,
led to the historical picture of *Clay on the Floor of the Senate*.
This composition includes portraits of distinguished senators
and civilians, skillfully and naturally grouped,—all in subordination to the main design. The Senate Chamber is
open to view, and the whole scene is represented with a
perfect fidelity, and with a vigor and breadth of effect

which, at once, attracts and enchains attention. In this, as
in all Col. STAUNTON's pictures, there appears a bold, as
well as a careful "handling," which suggests uncommon
manipulative power. Indeed, nearly all his pictures are
remarkable for strength, both in the treatment of his subject and in his manner of painting, which was most frank
and manly, and unfalteringly sustained. This quality, so
difficult to attain, he knew how to combine with the richest
color and the utmost delicacy and tenderness, as only genius
can. In color, Col. STAUNTON's pictures were, perhaps,
unusually warm and often brilliant, while yet harmonious,
even to softness.

But it was, as a religious painter, that Col. STAUNTON's
genius seemed to find most fitting exercise, and to promise
the richest results to the world. Among the most important
works of this character, were his *Walk to Emmaus*, where, in
the glowing haze of a Judean sunset, the heavenly and the
earthly types of humanity are most vividly and effectively
contrasted : *Casting out the Devils*, in which the Divine Christ
reveals his infinite power and majesty, in contrast with the
shrinking weakness of even his noblest followers, and where,
especially in the two possessed with evil spirits, are shown
a profound knowledge and accuracy in portraying the human figure, imparting to the picture great breadth of
expression and dramatic effect. But the greatest of his
finished productions is *The Ascension*, like the preceding,
a large-sized picture. In this, mystery is employed to
heighten the effect. The assembled disciples, most effectively grouped and individualized, are intently gazing into
the far depths of that luminous cloud ; or, according to
marked character, are rapt in all-absorbing thought, or

8

transported with overpowering emotion. That cloud, soft shaded, yet sun-bright with a glowing, supernatural radiance, tells of somewhat, far beyond what meets the eye: and so do the " two men in white apparel," as, half hovering, half resting down among the disciples, they seem self-poised in ether,—themselves almost as transparent and ethereal,—visible, yet spiritual,—the heavenly manifested to our earthly view. Yet all is in due subordination to the grand central idea,—the Son of God glorified. Two other great pictures remain unfinished,—*The Wise and Foolish Virgins*, and *Christ meeting Mary and Martha*. Indeed, great conceptions were thronging upon his mental vision.

To those privileged to enter it, his Studio seemed a sacred place, consecrated to lofty communings and beatific visions : where, in an atmosphere of pure spiritual ideals, his singularly beautiful person and noble face were often radiant with a light that seemed divine. In that presence, hundreds have stood, as it were, entranced, as they contemplated the sublimities of earth and heaven commingling in *The Ascension ;* or, as they hung upon the speaking lips of the risen Jesus in that evening walk, and, forgetting the paint and the canvas, have felt the scene realized before them. There was felt to be high Art ; there, an exemplification of the creative power of genius.

And now that Col. STAUNTON has sealed, with his life, his consecration to Art, in its highest form, who is there to stand up in his place ?—to take up the brush where he laid it down, and accomplish for the world what he would have accomplished ? Who, so inured to work, so intent upon improvement, so inflexibly and consistently devoted to the true, the beautiful, and the good, in all their forms,—so without a flaw in his character as a man,—so earnest as a Christian ?

A New York Artist friend thus writes : "No, I do not think it would be right to regard Col. STAUNTON as one whit less than a great Artist.   I have seen the works of our great painters often, and have thought about them a good deal. In religious painting, especially, I feel that we have lost more than we can know."

L.

POEMS BY E. M. O.

QUITO.

O, beauteous Earth! his worship dids't thou know,
  That thou shoulds't take him to thy very heart,
And set thy mountains, with their sun-kissed snow,
  To guard his precious dust, of thine a part?
Once to behold that vision of delight,
  To breathe the air of thine eternal Spring;—
And then, his soul, exultant, took its flight,
  To dwell, forever, with its Lord and King.
Grieve not, O, Earth! immortal was thy child,
  And, springing from his consecrated grave,*
Behold a Flower, whose splendor undefiled
  May yet thy darkened people cheer and save.
Its starry rays are lighted from above,
And, in its heart, the crimson Cross of Love.

SUBMISSION.

God keep us when, unwarned, the naked blade
Strikes home!
            On such a day, in dreamful quest,
She sat and counted weeks and fleeting months,
Until December's staunch and friendly winds
Should bring the wanderer home: and, at the thought,

---

* "Yonder city of Quito has stood over three hundred years, yet never has seen such a day as this,—the burial of a Protestant in a Protestant burial ground."—*Col. Staunton's Burial Service.*

The house with ruddy warmth was all aglow,
And, with light footsteps, up and down she went
Thro' all the quiet rooms. This, he would like,
This tint of wall, new-laid, this carved oak,—
These old-time favorite books, in gayer dress,
As if for welcome. All these home-sweet nooks,
Encloistered, fragrant with some dewy thought,
The darting sunbeam of swift love had found.
These pictures, over which his brooding soul
Had hung in rapture,—how their presence thrilled !
His life, by some mysterious power inwrought,
Moved her with such a glowing tenderness,
She turned to meet the answering smile and kiss.

" Good news ! good news !"
                    And, with the hurrying step
Of one who bears glad tidings from far seas,
The messenger sped on and found her there.

With eager fingers, trembling in their haste,
She tore the fluttering missive out, and read :

" Dear Madam,
                    This has been a sad, sad day,
For we have buried our beloved friend,
Your husband, in a foreign land."

                    No word,—
But sudden blindness, and the palsied hand,—
The death in death, slow ebbing into life,
With lengthened sighs and broken utterance,
And sobs that quickened, till the flood of tears
Swept the poor heart upon its Saviour's breast ;—
And, " Peace, be still," the surging billows calmed.

Then, with a majesty of grief, she rose
And went to do his bidding.

                    Gathering all
The precious children, given to her trust,
She told them, with a voice in which the chords
Of grief and joy in unison were touched,
How good it was to bear the heavy cross;
For, by her side, the blessed Jesus walked,
And, far above the toilsome, weary way,
An angel ever beckoned, on and on,
To that fair Mansion which had been prepared,
Before the world's foundation, for their rest.

A

SERMON

ON THE DEATH OF

MISS MARIETTA INGHAM,

ONE OF THE FOUNDERS OF INGHAM UNIVERSITY:

DELIVERED AT UNIVERSITY HALL, LE ROY,

JUNE 6th, 1867.

BY REV. WM. L. PARSONS, D. D.

9

SERMON.

Matt. 25 : 23.—" His lord said unto him, Well done, good and faithful servant; thou hast been faithful over a few things, I will make thee ruler over many things: enter thou into the joy of thy lord."

The fact that, in this world, we are on probation for another, that our eternal destiny of joy or of woe, of glory or of shame, is to depend upon the manner of our life here, is one of the most impressive which can address the human mind. The fact that no choice on the subject is left us; that the conditions of our being are such that probation, with its immeasurable results of happiness on the one hand or of misery on the other, is a necessity; that *neglect* to meet the issues which are upon us is as fatal as any positive transgression; that delay of retribution affords not even a shadow of hope for final impunity;—the fact that, unless righteous habits are formed as a shield against temptation, evil ones will surely fasten themselves upon us and ensure our ruin; that opportunities once disregarded never come back from the past to offer their advantages to us a second time;—these facts are full of startling solemnity to every thoughtful mind.

It must be the realization of these things which occasions such a universal outburst of joy in heaven over every sinner that turns from the error of his ways to the life of faith. And, doubtless, the most thrilling event possible in the his-

tory of a human soul is, that one should have successfully
endured to the end the tests of probation, and have been
called before the Great King, to hear from his lips, "Well
done, good and faithful servant; thou hast been faithful
over a few things, I will make thee ruler over many things:
enter thou into the joy of thy lord."

That the earthly life of any of us should have such glorious termination, we must be indebted solely to the grace
and mercy of our Lord Jesus Christ. But for the shedding
of his blood, the inspiration of his personal love and sympathy, the guidance of his Word and Spirit, the overrulings
of his providence, the ministry of the cross, and the loving
fellowship of an infinite Redeemer, not one of us would
ever wear the victor's crown.

And yet, the requirements of our probation are not un-
reasonable, and failure is without excuse.

The parable from which our text is taken corresponds in
its teachings with what we learn from reason and consciousness.

1. We are held responsible only for the exercise of such
gifts and talents as God has bestowed upon us. If we have
but one talent we are to give account for no more. If this
be of a particular type we are only required to make it fruitful in its own natural direction.

2. The service required of us is not some impossible task.
We are only to cultivate and put our powers to such duty
as waits about us on every hand. The particular manner
of employing them is not prescribed. The servants were
to have liberty to trade with their lord's capital in the way
most agreeable to themselves. No one was to be over-

burdened with responsibility; each was to serve "according to his several ability." Time also was given to develop and successfully use the talents: for it was only "after a long time," that the lord would return and call his servants to account.

3. The talents which God gives to men, moreover, are not dead, inanimate powers, into which we are required to infuse life. They are emphatically vital forces which will not, can not rest. Mind-powers are irresistibly self-active. And there is an infinitude of motive ever appealing to us to give them the right instead of the wrong direction.

4. We have but to use our talents aright, and success is certain. By exercise, they must grow. The two become four, the five increase to ten. It is not a question how much we gain by their use. The difference between the servants who were approved, and the one who was condemned was, that the former traded with their talents, while the latter simply refused to do so, and buried his lord's money in the earth. The reward was for the effort made to increase the capital with which each was entrusted. Those who had made it were the rightful heirs of the kingdom of heaven, whether they gained two talents or five; he who refused was deprived of his unoccupied talents, and was "cast into outer darkness, where there was weeping and gnashing of teeth."

5. Very abundant reward is ensured to those who use their talents aright. Employing them in the service of our Lord, under the inspiration of his infinite love, we become co-workers with him in the achievement of the richest

results ever to be garnered up in heaven; we come into fellowship with him in all the moral elements of his life and character; we gain the entire approbation of our reason and conscience, which is a blessing above all price; we overcome whatever is evil, and ally ourselves with all that is truly great and imperishably good: we reach the very sources of all true blessedness. In short, faithfulness over a *few* things here, makes us rulers over *many* hereafter. Nor does the diligent use of the talents merely double them. They will grow and multiply without end; and the results to ourselves and to others will be increasingly precious forever.

In view of these obvious instructions of the parable, the success of our probationary life ought not to be difficult or doubtful. That it is so, is a sad demonstration of the depth and the tenacity of human sinfulness; a mournful comment on the derangement of our mental and moral powers, and a startling illustration of the folly and peril of unbelief!

Our friend who has gone from us, and whose remains await their burial, has, we believe, made the great achievement;—has successfully finished her course, and has heard the sublime approval of her Judge: "Well done, good and faithful servant; thou hast been faithful over a few things: I will make thee ruler over many things."

We may then properly consider, *what were the talents which the Lord bestowed upon Miss Ingham; and how did she employ them?*

For the use of large accumulations of learning gained by educational advantages, she had no responsibility. These were not bestowed upon her. In the main, events, emergencies, experiences, were her text books, and she studied them well.

Her intellectual endowments were, in some respects at least, of a high order. She had a certain breadth and clearness of apprehension which enabled her to master the practical questions of life with singular correctness and success. Her mind was emphatically intuitive in its character; and although she could give cogent reasons for her conclusions, and often annihilate objections with a word, she seemed to see results directly in her premises, without the necessity of the logical process, to render them more obvious, so that, while seeming to jump at her conclusions, she could always indicate her reasoning processes. Her mind was strikingly active. There was no necessity for a great occasion to call out her powers. Her intellect seemed to be constituted with an inherent impulse towards perpetual activity. It would probably be difficult to find one waking hour from cradle to coffin when her mind was not more or less vigorously exercised.

Nor was her intellect of that narrow cast which sees only one way of achieving results. She had great versatility of thinking, and could easily determine whether a given course was possible or impossible, wise or unwise, and whether it would be fruitful or barren of desirable consequences. If the ordinary methods of accomplishing results were, in any case, encompassed with difficulty, she was not baffled. Another power of her mind came at once into play,—her invention;—and she would find out a way of her own, and then bring the powers of nature to co-operate with her in carrying it into execution.

Nor was she visionary or impracticable in her attempts to

adapt means to ends. She could execute as well as plan,—and while she was eminently practical, her genius was not of that narrow and unsatisfactory sort which is contented with getting things barely and baldly done. There was room, and, indeed, a strong demand in her intellectual being for the exercise of taste, and a reach after the ideal in the manner of her doing. She would, as far as possible, put a clothing of beauty upon the most common routine operations. The beauty of things, to her mind, was a part of their practical effectiveness.

It was another marked feature of Miss Ingham's mind, that it was eminently progressive. She had none of that slow and doubtful conservatism which prevents many minds from marching forward with the growth of knowledge and the unfolding of events. No present achievements satisfied her. Her plans penetrated the future as naturally as the present. It mattered nothing to her that things had been done in a given way from time immemorial, if that way were not the *best*. The new, to her, was better than the old unless the old could prove itself better than new. Improvement was to her mind a matter of course,—a necessity.

Miss Ingham had a mind greedy of knowledge. Few persons of either sex apply themselves more diligently, and few better understand current events, the world over. Intuitively, she apprehended the social, political and moral influences which are at work in the world, and easily referred the on-going changes in human history to their legitimate causes. Any kind or degree of knowledge which was needful to her she easily gained. When, twenty years ago, her physicians despaired of her life and gave her up to die, she at once grappled with the difficult problems of medical science, and soon became her own most successful practitioner.

As to Miss INGHAM's emotional endowment, less can, and less need be said. To a certain extent, this great function of her mind seemed merged, as it were, in her intellectual being. That carried, in itself, the forces which, in other minds, are found largely in the sensibility. Her feelings were scarcely distinguishable from her thoughts. There was a marvelous intimacy between her intellect and her will. Her thoughts were no sooner in her consciousness, than her will was all astir to execute them. She, perhaps, never in her life waited an hour to be pressed into action by the mere impulse of her emotional nature. She rarely analyzed her emotions or inquired for their dictation in practical matters. To *know* what should be done, was, with her, to do it.

In cases where it was specially pertinent that the feelings should lead the will in its activities, she showed as ready and as mercurial a sensibility as any one. When the cause of suffering humanity presented itself, the responses of her heart were prompt and characteristic. Indeed, the fact that her sensibility was not under the pressure and friction of incessant appeal, gave to her emotions, whenever any special circumstances called them forth, a force and freshness which were delightful. I have never seen more genuine manifestations of *pleasure*, than in her, when destroying the note of some old pupil whose misfortunes had destroyed her ability to meet her obligations. Perhaps no citizen could be found among us during the late war whose sensibilities were more profoundly or purely stirred by the sorrows of the suffering than were hers.

10

But the characteristic talent with which she was endowed is found in her will. Her executive ability was remarkable. There was a kind of authority and force about her volitions which necessitated their being *felt*. Her choices and determinations were made potent, not by the strength of the language which expressed and conveyed them, nor by any outside demonstration, but by the simple native force inherent in her spirit itself. Her will was regal by nature. This will-power was not merely executive through her own organism alone, but it penetrated other minds and applied itself to other hands and other instruments than her own, with a quiet and masterly effectiveness. If she had been gifted with a genius for inspiring others with a high degree of enthusiasm and of affection, as she was for impressing her volitions upon them, she would have made her purposes felt far and wide as great formative forces in society.

Her will-power was of that strong type which gives little heed to obstacles. She had a real pleasure in ruling them out of the way. Nor was her power of that unbalanced sort which achieves a great victory in one direction, and, at the same time, yields to a trifling temptation to self-indulgence in another. It was not vigorous one day, and vacillating the next. It was not strong to accomplish the ends of self-interest, and ineffective towards the ends of righteousness. She knew nothing of *resolutions* to do, without the *doing*. The stream of executive force from her nature would flow on, in its great channels, around or over the obstructions, till it reached the sea of accomplishment. There was a *cling* to her will, which seemed like the adherence of the laws of nature to the materials on which they act. It was such an all-pervading element in her whole personality, that to be in her presence while her mind was engaged in its executive operations, without feeling, by sympathy, the intensity of her will-power acting upon one's own spirit, was impossible.

Her moral and her religious nature corresponded with her mental. With such an intellect, she could scarcely fail clearly to discriminate the moral qualities of acts and principles. The right, to her mind, had its emblem in the noon-day sun; the wrong, in the rayless darkness of midnight: justice was seated on the throne of God; injustice made the lake of fire where dwell the devil and his angels. Her conscience held unbroken sway in her voluntary nature. Her moral feelings, too, were intense. She was a good hater of evil, and her indignation at wrong doing was often withering. Her sense of righteous obligation, her reverence for God and duty, her appreciation of truth, her pleasure in whatever was morally beautiful and of good report, in whatever was noble and generous and self-sacrificing. were eminently worthy of her and of the moral constitution God had given her.

Her natural affections were, in the highest degree, strong and beautiful. The world will never know with what tender solicitude and practical devotion she cared for her earthly kindred, and for the pupils committed to her charge.

Such, as we understand the facts, were the talents which our Heavenly Father gave to our departed friend.

How did she improve them?

It is not necessary to assume that she was faultless in the use of these powers. She was more sensible of her own imperfections than were any of her friends. Indeed, as a general principle, it is found quite true that persons of decided characteristics, of positive qualities, do exhibit striking mistakes and faults in attempting to carry into execution the very best principles which they apprehend and essentially follow. The strongest minds are exposed to corresponding weaknesses and infirmities. It is not pretended that Miss INGHAM was exempt from this common fact of human nature. Certainly, she did not commit the unpardonable mistake of burying her talents: she vigorously used them.

Miss INGHAM began life at the opening of the present century, at Saybrook, Conn., the daughter of Amasa and Mary Ingham. She was the oldest of seven daughters, in a family of fourteen children. While yet a child, she became an effective co-laborer with her mother in the hard work of caring for that populous household. Scarcely more than a score of years had elapsed, when that excellent mother passed on to her grave; and upon this daughter there was devolved the excessive burden of her own and her mother's responsibilities. Thus, from very early life, she necessarily formed habits of industrious effort in behalf of others.

Some nine years earlier than the death of her mother, when she was but twelve years of age, an unusual event transpired in that family. The twin daughters, Emily and Julia, were born. Fearing she might not live, the mother deliberately and formally gave the child Emily to her daughter Marietta, to be her child,—to be, by her, provided for, trained up, educated; and the child Julia, to another daughter, who not long after passed away. The mother recovered her health, but she did not take back the sacred gift, which, in the fear of God and in the expectation of death, she had bestowed upon this child of twelve years. She had been led to it by her heavenly Guide; she had done it in his name, and with confidence that he would, in some way, be glorified by her seemingly unmotherly act.

And now I seem to see that, on this providential act of that mother, away back in the early part of the century, great changes and results were suspended. That circumstance involved Ingham University, with all its history, and the fruits of its labors, past, present, and to come.

That living, immortal gift, received into the heart of one possessed of the marked qualities already considered, was a telling event, and its momentous responsibility was duly realized. She must be not only sister, but mother, to her new charge. All her feelings of obligation, of solicitude, of affection, of hope and fear, were aroused; and her whole being vibrated and responded to new and higher springs of action. For nine years, this sister-mother, oftener than she looked upon the face of the little one, was musing over the thought, *" the child is mine;"* and then, as her own mother passed on to her heavenly home, the responsibility of caring for the precious gift was all her own.

As soon as she could be spared from the homestead, she went her way alone, and entered upon her life-work. At once, she engaged in a business for which her natural taste and genius admirably fitted her, and soon accumulated sufficient means to carry her plans into execution.

Her first purpose, to which all her movements were made subservient, was to secure a complete education to her sister-daughter. She liberally aided her other sisters also in gaining their education, and contributed largely to

help a brother in the prosecution of his studies for the
Christian ministry.

After the education of her daughter was finished, a new
turn was given to her affairs. She had educated her child
for Christ, and for practical usefulness in the world: and
now, she was ready to go about her Master's work. While
in the process of her education, she had become a Christian,
and her heart had gained an outlook toward the dark places
of Greece for a field of missionary labor.

But the heart of this sister-*mother* was touched, and her
whole being quivered with the feeling that she could not be
separated from her child. What was to be done? Her
ready mind soon solved the problem; a compromise might
be made. Our country had a mission for the world, and the
Great West was, ere long, to shape the destiny of America.
What better or more promising field of usefulness could be
opened for the dear laborer she had prepared for the Lord's
harvest!

"Let us," she said, "go West, and build up an institution
to educate young women for God and duty, as you have
been educated. I will go with you, and will put all my
means into *this* missionary enterprise. I will give *my* life
to the business part, while you consecrate yours to the
school proper: and so you will do the world more good
than if you leave me, to toil alone in a foreign land." The
proposition seemed to come down from above, and was, at
length, cheerfully accepted.

They started for Illinois, but were induced to stop in
Western New York. Thirty-two years ago, their grand
purpose was entered upon in Attica, where a destitute and
promising field seemed waiting, and where they labored

successfully some two years. Then, in 1837, a few enterprising and appreciative gentlemen of Le Roy, held out
strong inducements for the removal of their establishment,
which were accepted.   And Ingham University is the result
of the labor, for a score and a half of years, of those hands
and of that heart which sleep in death to-day.

I need not say how diligently and faithfully these sisters
have wrought in this community.   They consecrated themselves and their work, with deepest sincerity, to God, who,
it cannot be doubted, will say of the work and of the
workers, *"well done."*

The two sisters who belonged so emphatically to each
other, brought with them other sisters, also, as co-laborers,
whose earnest devotion to the common work demands
grateful and honorable recognition.   Two of these lie in
the consecrated burial place on the University grounds,
whither our footsteps will follow our dead to-day.

Here, then, is the life-work and the lasting monument
of our departed friend.   Upon this she employed all her
talents, and with a singleness of devotion, as perfect as it
was beautiful.   The *Institution*, the *Institution*, the good it
was doing and might do, was her life.

The inquiry may arise, has she done all for Christ?   Did
she employ her talents truly in the service of him who gave
them to her, or did she use them for a selfish end?   Was it
to accumulate wealth and honor for herself, or to extend the
kingdom of her Redeemer?

I believe her direct consciousness was, that she labored
incessantly, and with her whole heart, for the Institution,
whose vital forces were scarcely separable from those of her
own inmost heart and life.   And to the question, "why am

I toiling, with every power of my being and to the latest breath of my life, to build up this educational establishment?"—I believe her deeper consciousness would, at every moment, have responded, "that good may be done; that young women may be educated for usefulness; that the world may be made better; that Christ may be glorified." And this is the Christian response, the very one which will bring back the echo from heaven, "Well done, good and faithful servant; thou hast been faithful over a few things, I will make thee ruler over many things: enter thou into the joy of thy Lord."

That money-making, for its own sake, was not her object, is sufficiently obvious from the original consecration of all her capital to the work, and from the fact that substantially all her gains, from year to year, have been expended to increase the capacity and usefulness of this educational establishment.

From the earliest periods of her life, the lessons of economy were forced upon her, until that virtue became with her an habitual and conscientious principle of action. The providence as well as the lips of Christ had taught her to "gather up the fragments that nothing be lost." If it was the characteristic habit of her life to make all things tell, to the utmost, toward her great object in living, it was to her *praise;* and well were it for the world, if her example, in this respect, were better heeded.

But Miss INGHAM's work is done. One has judged it in infinite wisdom, and has, doubtless, given it his loving approval. She has done more than the wise woman of Solomon, who "built her own house," for she has built a house not for herself alone, but for her race; not for her personal enjoyment, but for the glory of God. Many will rise up to call her blessed. Few of the four thousand who have enjoyed the advantages of this school, will fail, on hearing of her departure, to bless her for the work she has done. Scores of young women who have been her beneficiaries will thank God for her liberality to them; and many who have here learned to love and follow Christ, will especially magnify the Lord for what this Christian woman has accomplished. Numbers there were who penetrated her inner life and discovered her deeper springs of action, and such will remember her reverently and tenderly for some elements of character, which, seen by others only at the surface, were by them misapprehended. And will she not be specially honored by thoughtful men and women for the noble example she has set to her sex, in putting her weak woman's hand to a great needed Christian enterprise, and in carrying it through, by the heroism and force of her own spirit, all unaided by such accumulations of capital and influence from others as are usually demanded for such establishments? Such an example seems peculiarly valuable at this period of the world's history when so many providential combinations of events are calling loudly upon *woman* to do with her great might, what she can possibly find to do for the salvation of mankind. Miss INGHAM's intuitive apprehension of the wants of the world and of her country, placed her in the van of this detachment of the army of progress.

Many will desire to know something of Miss INGHAM's religious experience, and it is not inappropriate that it should come into view on this occasion.

Natural characteristics must show themselves in all the

11

phases of the outward life; and the peculiar type of Miss
INGHAM's mind at once suggests the leading features of her
Christian character. Her religion would manifest itself
chiefly in her intellect and will. Her feeling would be so
mingled with her thinking and acting, as to be scarcely distinguishable from them in her consciousness. Her deep
sense of the holiness of God and of the necessity of intrinsic
righteousness, together with that conscious want of it in
herself which the best Christians experience, naturally put
her spirit under the influence of *fear* that she could not be
accepted, rather than encouraged that *joyous hope* which it
is the privilege of the Christian to cherish. With her
peculiar constitution of mind and with her early Puritan
instruction, which was somewhat emphatically of the legal
kind, lastingly impressed upon her, it is not strange that
she was a severe critic upon herself and her spiritual attainments. She often earnestly craved an experience of religious joy, of which her nature and her habits of mind would
scarcely admit. In common with large numbers of Christian
people, she was under the pernicious impression that her
religious character was determined by her emotions, not
recognizing the truth that religious *feelings* alone are by no
means the best tests of the Christian hope. The Bible does
not encourage a reliance upon them, as upon doing the will
of God and choosing the right. Measuring herself by this
false standard, Miss INGHAM was distrustful, often painfully
so, of her religious experience. But, if using her talents
with unceasing fidelity for her Lord and Master, made her
a Christian; if to *love* the Lord, is to keep his command-
ments; if gladly to give the cup of cold water to a disciple
in the name of the Master; if tenderly to regard the church

of Christ, and tenaciously to adhere to perceived religious duty; if a conscious preference and prayer to be like Christ herself and to have every one else so; if a relish for the most spiritual truths of the gospel : if to ·· call upon the name of the Lord ¨ in the accents of the little child; if such things are in the line of Christian experience and of a "good hope through grace," then was Miss INGHAM, emphatically and eminently, a Christian.   That such facts habitually entered into her religious life, is well known to all who were intimately acquainted with her.

With her practical, working mind, to do the will of God, when apprehended, was so in consonance with her very nature, that doing it seemed rather a natural than a religious exercise.   And in truth, the more *naturally* we do the will of God, the more genuine and acceptable is the service. Her "doubts" were all of that sort which the old divines were accustomed to set down as the most satisfactory proofs of the Christian state.   It was herself she doubted, not her Saviour.   The deepest convictions of her nature were, that God lives and reigns; that he is the rewarder of them that diligently seek him ; that the Bible, which was her daily counselor and the stay of her life, contains the revelation of his will ; that salvation is attainable alone through the atonement and righteousness of Christ.   On that Saviour's mercy and loving kindness toward sinners, Miss INGHAM cast herself nearly forty years ago, when a resident of Pittsfield, Mass.   And, surely, she has to-day found his word verified : "and him that cometh unto me I will in no wise cast out."

The type of her experience, so far as we could know, did not change in the final crisis.   She saw no gathering group of angels; the heavens did not visibly open upon her vision

and send down their light on the dark valley through which
she was passing; seraph voices did not salute her expiring
senses with the music of the heavenly world; but, true to
herself and to God, while her suffering was greatest, she
asked no more than this: "Father, if it be possible, let this
cup pass from me; nevertheless not as I will, but as thou
wilt." On Sabbath evening, she said to me, "I would not,
if I could, have it otherwise than my Heavenly Father ap-
points:" and so, I doubt not, she would have said, if her
agony had equaled, in her measure, that of her sympathizing
Redeemer, when, in his own death, made so afflictive, in
order that he might succor his most tried disciples, he
exclaimed, almost in the accents of despair, "My God, my
God, why hast thou forsaken me."

But what a touching illustration of her unselfish thoughtfulness of others, were those almost last words, when she
called her weary watchers to her bedside and bade them go
and take some rest. Surely hers was a death, in which, as
the Scripture hath said, "the Lord taketh pleasure."

It was fitting, yea, it was beautiful, that she should now
be called home. Her race was run; her three score years
and ten were nearly reached; her life-work was accomplished, and could easily be taken up and borne along by
younger and stronger hands: her worn frame, her trembling
limbs, her exhausted bodily powers, were entitled to the
repose of the Christian's grave; while her soul was, doubtless, ready for its birth into the heavenly life, into the
family of the redeemed above, the general assembly of the
church of the First Born. Earth could spare her; heaven
was ready to hail her coming. It is not as if she had gone
down in mid-ocean, with her life-work but half accomplished.

She had made the voyage over the troubled sea, and outrode all the storms of life; she had come in sight of the haven, and why should she not enter the heavenly port, fold up the canvas of the earthly life, drop her anchor and be forever at rest ?

> "Thou art gone to the grave; but we will not deplore thee,
> For God was thy ransom, thy Guardian and Guide;
> He gave thee, He took thee, and He will restore thee;
> And death has no sting, for the Saviour hath died."

And, now, what are the lessons of this occasion? Miss INGHAM, "being dead, yet speaketh." And what is her message to us all to-day? What, to these beloved pupils gathered into the Institution she has so fondly loved?—what, to the thousands of young ladies who have gone forth from these halls in past years, and who are, to-day, fighting the great battle of life?—what, to the citizens of Le Roy, among whom she has so long dwelt and labored, and who have intimately known her manner of life?—what, especially, to the women of this assembly and of this generation? Is it not this? *Use your talents for God and mankind;—use them all, earnestly and without ceasing?* This, surely, was the lesson of her life.

And, with this never-to-be-forgotten hour, there comes, as it seems to me, to these beloved kindred and personally afflicted friends, a precious lesson. You need not that I should express it for your instruction, but I know you will allow me the pleasure of doing it for my own gratification, and for that of the multitude of your sympathizing friends. It is a lesson of joy in sorrow.

Viewed from the earthward side, the passing away of such a spirit, from such fidelities of love and labor; the closing of a life which, without cessation, for two-thirds of a century, has been so crowded with generous and true-hearted efforts to bless her kindred and the world, suggests the drapery of deepest sorrow and mourning. And especially is that drapery suggested to you, dear Madam, whom, to the hour of her death she sacredly carried in her heart of hearts, with more, if possible, than the fidelity and affection of a mother.

But, viewed on the heavenward side, the whole scene changes. The clouds and darkness, the sin and chastenings of the earthly state, are passed away forever: the burdens and anxieties of probation are all over. She has gone home, and heard the "Well done" of her Lord and King above; she has entered upon higher and more inspiring fidelities and honors in God's kingdom of universal truth and love. "Faithful here over a *few* things," she has gone to be a ruler there over *many* things,—to exert a grander sweep of influence, with correspondingly glorious results.

And does not all this suggest to you an experience into which shall enter, at least, a large element of holy joy and praise? You shared with her here, all her trials and sorrows; and, certainly, you may share with her, now, her joy which is unspeakable and full of glory. And I know of no way in which her usefulness can be more surely perpetuated, or your courage to labor on in the good work she has left behind can be more delightfully increased and strengthened, than by a rich baptism of the heavenly bliss which, to-day, thrills the heart of the dear departed.

The sublimest of all earthly experiences is that deep, holy joy which the Christian heart may cherish, at the moment when the spirit is bowed down under the weight of an overwhelming bereavement.

> " When the wounds of woe are healing,
>   When the heart is all resigned,
>   'Tis the solemn feast of feeling,
>   'Tis the Sabbath of the mind."

LETTER OF DR. J. C. GALLUP.

CLINTON, JULY 20, 1867.

MRS. E. E. INGHAM STAUNTON:

My Dear Sister:—I feel, this morning, very much inclined to write you a few words relative to the Christian character of your departed sister. Since her death, it has often occurred to me that hers was one of those phases of Christian experience more liable to be misapprehended than almost any other, so accustomed are we to be guided, in forming our estimates of Christian experience, by the rule that "out of the abundance of the heart, the *mouth* speaketh." True, she was a marked representative of the class of Christians known as Marthas, and was, from her very girlhood, "cumbered with much serving." Yet, during her long and active life, she never found time to devote to fashionable display, worldly pleasure, or the accumulation of wealth for her own sake. Left, at an early age, with the care of a large family of motherless sisters, she devoted herself with a degree of energy and sagacity to their intellectual and religious training, rarely, if ever, surpassed. And immediately, upon their arrival at the age of maturity, she entered upon the vastly responsible work, at that time almost untried by her sex, to which she consecrated the remainder of her days.

She was not one of those referred to by the Saviour, who were continually crying, "Lord, Lord," &c. But none can

12

point to the time, during all those years of toil, that she was not earnestly striving to do the will of the Father.

Never has it been my pleasure to know one well, who could more consistently and appropriately adopt the language of that most practical of all the sacred authors, the Apostle James, "Show me thy faith without thy works, and I will show you my faith by my works."

Few, perhaps, if any, knew better than myself the inward experiences of her earlier Christian life. The first time that, in the presence of others, I ever knelt before God and attempted to pray, was at her side: and after she had first addressed the Mercy Seat on my behalf. And from that time on for years, she and myself were accustomed to a very free interchange of thought and feeling relative to our Christian growth and enjoyment.

Although constitutionally distrustful of her own spiritual experiences, she was foremost in everything that was calculated to promote the religious interests of others. In setting apart so generous a portion of her means for the education of her brother for the ministry, in her zeal for the cause of Sabbath Schools and Missions, her ever ardent desire for revivals of religion, and her love for those most earnest and successful in promoting them, in her love for the Sanctuary,—in her solicitude that the Institution, for which the world is so largely indebted to her, at its foundation, and during all its subsequent history, should be everywhere known as based upon and permeated by the principles and spirit of the gospel, I see out-cropping the evidences of that inner life, often hidden, I doubt not, from herself even, but known ever to Him "whose eye seeth every secret thing." But her sleepless spirit has ceased from its activi-

ties, and her limbs, never weary in running upon errands of
mercy to others, are now at rest. Oh! that I could have
witnessed the first breaking of the light of the celestial city
upon the vision of her released spirit!—and her gratified
astonishment, as in heavenly accents, the Saviour said:
" Inasmuch as ye have done it unto the least of these, ye
have done it unto me."

EXTRACT FROM AN ADDRESS BEFORE THE ALUMNÆ.

Unselfishness! I have purposely left this attribute to the last, thinking to exemplify it in the character of the honored friend who has so recently left us and passed into that kingdom where, we are taught, there are no ways hedged up, and she will find full scope for all her powers. I would not assume to take upon myself the honor of speaking her praise or setting forth her virtues. I would simply draw one lesson from her life, that ours may be enriched. That you

> "May learn how mortals, frail as we,
> Fared on beneath the storm and sun,
> Until a crown eternally
> By the brief march of life was won."

A singularly unselfish woman. Never dreaming, herself, of practicing anything like self-indulgence, she could not understand it in others, and looked upon it with a loathing such as only those can comprehend who have habitually gathered up and held in leash all passions and desires,—subject in all things to reason and "abstinence divine." With her, the veil of the temple—that is, the *flesh*—was rent, and self—huge, gluttonous, insatiate *self*—was completely vanquished, swallowed up in the universal weal or woe. And this, not alone in her maturity, after youthful fancies had lost their zest,

> " But, in the greener blossom of her life,
> Ere the full blade caught flower, and when time gave
> Respite, she did not slacken soul nor sleep,
> But, with great hand and heart wrought good for man
> Out of sharp straits and many a grievous thing."

I wish, my sisters, that you would remember this, and
tell it to your children and to *their* children, that there once
lived, in the halls of your Alma Mater,—who, in fact, reared
those very halls,—a woman, little in stature, but *so strong in
will* that she conquered herself.

      *   *   *   *   *   *   *

Most truly was she one of those,

> " ——who have lived out all the length of all their years ; who
> Blameless,   *   *   *   *   *
> And without shame and without fear, have wrought
> Things memorable, and, while their days held out,
> In sight of all men and the sun's great light,
> Have got them glory and given of their own praise
> To the earth that bare them, and the day that bred
> Home friends and far off hospitalities.
>
>   *   *   *   *   *   *   *
>
> But when white age and venerable death
> Mow down the strength and life within their limbs,
> Drain out the blood and darken their clear eyes,
> Immortal power is on them, having past
> Through splendid life, and death desirable,
> To the clear seat and remote throne of souls,—
> Lands undiscoverable in the far off West,
> Round which, the strong stream of a sacred sea
> Rolls without wind-power ; and the snow
> There shows not her white wings and windy feet.
> Nor thunder, nor swift rain saith anything,
> Nor the sun burns, but all things rest and thrive."

ALUMNA.

www.ingramcontent.com/pod-product-compliance
Lightning Source LLC
Chambersburg PA
CBHW020039030726
47499CB00007B/2496